W9-APF-203

Keep Ms. Sugarman in the Fourth Grade

Also by Elizabeth Levy
Published by HarperCollins*Publishers*
FRANKENSTEIN MOVED IN ON THE FOURTH FLOOR
DRACULA IS A PAIN IN THE NECK

Keep Ms. Sugarman in the Fourth Grade

by Elizabeth Levy

illustrated by Dave Henderson

HarperCollins*Publishers*

Library of Congress Cataloging-in-Publication Data
Levy, Elizabeth.
  Keep Ms. Sugarman in the fourth grade / by Elizabeth Levy ; illustrated by Dave Henderson.
      p.   cm.
  Summary: Jackie, who has always had trouble in school, begins to develop more self-confidence under the guidance of her fourth-grade teacher and is crushed when Ms. Sugarman is promoted to principal in the middle of the school year.
  ISBN 0-06-020426-5. — ISBN 0-06-020427-3 (lib. bdg.)
  [1. Schools—Fiction. 2. Teacher-student relationships—Fiction. 3. Self-Confidence—Fiction.] I. Henderson, Dave, ill. II. Title.
PZ7.L5827Ke 1992   91-22576
[Fic]—dc20   CIP
                                                              AC

To the real Dr. Ruth Sugarman. My handwriting is still lousy and I never learned to spell, but the confidence that you gave me was the best lesson I ever learned.

To the many inspiring elementary school teachers I have met in my travels. You never give up on your kids and you still delight in the funny poem, the incredible drawing. All of you leave behind someone like me and Jackie who will never forget you.

Contents

Keep Ms. Sugarman in the Fourth Grade

1

Smart—Not Smart-Alecky

"That's for nothing, Jackie. Wait till you do something," my dad said as he kissed me on the cheek. It wasn't the first time he'd said that. Very few things get said around our house for the first time.

Mom put bowls of homemade granola in front of us. "I've changed the recipe, Joe. Tell me what you think of it," she said.

"Sure, Margaret," said Dad. He winked at me. Neither of us loves granola. "So today's the first day of the fourth grade," he said, "the year they separate the sheep from the goats."

"Baaa!" I bleated.

"That's what a sheep does," said Dad. "A goat goes 'naaa.'"

"Are you calling me a goat?" I asked him.

"Naaa!" said Dad. He laughed, but I didn't think it was funny. I was in no mood for jokes. My new fourth-grade teacher, Ms. Sugarman, had the reputation for being the toughest teacher in the school. It wasn't as if school had been a roaring success in my life so far.

I was more like Mom's granola. Every teacher tinkered with the recipe, but so far nobody loved the result. My kindergarten teacher thought I interrupted story hour too much. My first-grade teacher worried about my hand-eye coordination—just because I kept letting the class frog out of the aquarium. I was into animal rights before my time. In second grade Mr. Chow thought I had too much energy for my own good. In third grade the principal, Dr. Vargas, talked my parents into having me tested to see if I was hyperactive. I got lucky. The tester said that I was "within the normal range."

"Is it better to be a sheep or a goat?" I asked Dad. I kind of meant it as a serious

2

question, but the words came out of my mouth sounding sassy.

Dad twisted his spoon between his thumb and forefinger, rapping out a tattoo on the edge of his bowl.

"Goats are nothing but trouble," he said. "When people make fun of you, you're the goat. Goats get butted around a lot."

I took a bite of the granola, shifting my weight in my chair.

"Stop fidgeting," Mom said to me. I sat still.

We finished breakfast, and Dad gave me another kiss.

"Seriously, Jackie," said Dad, "this year I want you to apply yourself. Fourth grade is important. It's not just fun and games."

"I bet parents all over the country are saying that to fourth graders this morning," I said.

"Don't be smart with your dad, young lady," warned Mom.

"I thought that was what you wanted," I said, "for me to be smart."

"Smart, not smart-alecky," said Dad. "It's time you learned the difference." Dad is a police officer, and every once in a while he gets this "voice of authority."

Mom works as a secretary. She got really good grades in school. Dad didn't.

"You always say that 'school smart' doesn't add up to a hill of beans in the real world," I said to Dad.

Dad glared at me. "That's a good example of smart-alecky," he warned me.

I didn't talk back, because I knew this time Dad was right. Smart kids get good grades. Smart-alecky kids get in trouble. I guess goats are smart-alecky. I think I like goats better, even if they do say "naaa." It's better than "baa."

2

Was That Supposed to Be Funny?

Ms. Sugarman is short and a little dumpy. She certainly isn't young. She's got hair with a lot of gray in it. I like young teachers the best, funny ones with a lot of energy. Ms. Sugarman doesn't look like she could run around the block.

She wrote her name on the board. "As if we all don't know who she is," I whispered to my friend Shannon. "Shh," said Shannon.

Ms. Sugarman turned around. "Did anybody say anything?" she asked.

I folded my hands on top of my desk.

"Good morning, girls and boys," she said in that singsong voice that teachers always use.

"Good morning, Ms. Sugarman," we said in unison.

"Welcome to the fourth grade," she said.

"Where they separate the sheep from the goats," I blurted out. That's me, old motor mouth.

"Who said that?" Ms. Sugarman asked.

"Jackie!" said Seth Matthews. Seth Matthews is neat, clean, smart, and obnoxious.

Ms. Sugarman smiled. "Sheep from the goats, eh?" she said. "What does that mean, Jackie?"

I shrugged. "It's just something people say," I said.

"But what does it mean?"

"I don't know," I admitted. "My dad said it to me."

Ms. Sugarman walked down the aisle and stood in front of my desk. I couldn't believe that I was in trouble already.

"Look it up, and report to me tomorrow," said Ms. Sugarman.

"Look it up where?" I asked.

Ms. Sugarman smiled at me. "You're in fourth grade now," she said. "You should know how to use the library, right?"

"Naaa," I said softly.

Ms. Sugarman heard me. "Are you a goat?" she asked.

I shrugged.

"Don't shrug," said Ms. Sugarman.

"Yes, Ma'am," I said.

I slunk down farther in my seat.

"I'll help you," whispered Shannon.

"Jackie needs all the help in the world," sneered Seth. Adam laughed. Adam is kind of Seth Matthews's parrot. He laughs at *anything* Seth says, no matter how dumb.

"Shut up," said Shannon.

"What was that?" Ms. Sugarman asked.

Now I had gotten Shannon in trouble too, and we were only about five minutes into fourth grade.

"Nothing, Ms. Sugarman," I said quickly. "I was just coughing."

"I never heard a cough that sounded like 'Jackie needs all the help in the world,'" said Ms. Sugarman. She stared at Seth, who squirmed in his chair. Seth *never* gets in trouble.

"Was that supposed to be funny, Seth?" Ms. Sugarman asked.

Seth didn't answer.

"I like to laugh," said Ms. Sugarman, "so if that was a joke, please explain it to me." She wasn't smiling. It was kind of hard to believe that she liked to laugh.

"Seth," said Ms. Sugarman, "do you have something funny to say to the whole class?"

Seth shook his head. He examined his fingernails, and his fingernails were always clean.

"Girls and boys," said Ms. Sugarman, "nothing pleases me more than to be made to laugh, but you can't laugh *at* each other. That is a rule. Does everybody understand?"

We all nodded, but I had a feeling it wasn't going to be easy to make Ms. Sugarman laugh.

3

What Did the Goats Do Wrong?

Shannon and I went to the library. "I need a book about sheep and goats," I said to Ms. Tegen, our librarian. She's a lot younger than Ms. Sugarman and easier to talk to.

Shannon got a book about goats. I got a book about sheep. Mine was way too long. It was about a hundred pages, and it looked as though it had been written in the last century.

"I'll be in fifth grade before I finish this," I said. I looked at the pictures. It showed people in Australia shearing sheep.

"Look at this," said Shannon. "People drink goat's milk."

"They drink sheep's milk too," I said. "It sounds disgusting."

"Maybe that's where the saying comes from," said Shannon. "I bet sheep's milk is better than goat's milk."

"They both sound yucky. I wouldn't want goat's milk on *my* granola."

I took the books back to Ms. Tegen. "Don't you have *one* book about sheep *and* goats?" I asked her.

Ms. Tegen handed me a book on mammals—*Aardvarks to Zebras.*

"I'm getting nowhere," I muttered to Shannon.

"You could write about Noah's Ark," said Shannon.

"Sorry, Ms. Sugarman, I couldn't do my homework—I lost it in the flood," I said.

Shannon giggled. I was glad I could make her laugh, but it wouldn't keep me from flunking out of fourth grade on the first day.

I took the library books back up to the desk. "That was quick," said Ms. Tegen. "I'm glad I was able to help."

I didn't have the heart to tell her that she hadn't.

I went home in a lousy mood.

Mom got home around five thirty. She took one look at me and knew that something was wrong. I hate that, even when she's right.

"Jackie?" she asked. "Didn't you like your new teacher?"

"I'm in trouble with Ms. Sugarman already," I told her. "I got extra homework on the first day."

Mom sighed. "Oh no, Jackie. Fourth grade is really important. You should have started out on the right foot."

I was mad that she immediately thought I was to blame. "It's not my fault," I yelled. "It's Dad's."

"What does your father have to do with it?" Mom asked.

"He called me a goat," I muttered.

"He didn't," said Mom. "Who said you were a goat? I'll talk to them."

"Dad called me a goat at breakfast," I insisted. "You heard him." Sometimes Mom remembers only what she wants to remember.

"Your father was just speaking metaphorically. He wants you to do well this year, just as I do. And now you're in trouble the very first day."

"Please, Mom, it's not that big a deal. I'm not really in trouble. I just don't know how to separate sheep from goats."

"Oh, you mean like in the Bible," said Mom.

I stared at her. "You mean that's where it comes from?" I couldn't believe that Mom had the answer for me, just like that. A whole library couldn't help me, and Mom could. "The Bible talks about sheep and goats?" I asked.

"Sure," said Mom. "Jesus was explaining that on Judgment Day the righteous would be separated from the sinners, like a shepherd divides his sheep from the goats."

"What did the goats do wrong?" I asked. It didn't sound fair to me.

"I'm sure that's not what Jesus meant," said Mom. "He was a shepherd himself, so he spoke simply."

Mom got our Bible and showed it to me. There it was in Matthew in black and white.

"Thanks, Mom," I said. "That helps. I got

to go do my homework."

Dad came in just at that moment. "How're my girls?" he asked.

"Fine," I said.

"Jackie's got a lot of homework," said Mom.

"Great, it's about time. Jackie needs some discipline." He gave me a kiss. "So how was the first day of the fourth grade?"

I looked at Mom. I didn't want her to tell Dad that I had *extra* work.

Mom closed the Bible. "Go do your work, honey," she said. "I'll call you for dinner."

I went up to my room. I'm not a very good writer. My handwriting's crummy, and my spelling's even worse. I started to write an essay about sheep and goats. It was boring. I tore it up.

Then I began to write—something completely different. I was so engrossed in what I was doing that I didn't even hear Mom call me for dinner—and that's not like me at all.

4

Naaa

"Here," I said to Ms. Sugarman. I shoved my folded-up yellow-lined paper onto her desk.

"What's this?" Ms. Sugarman asked.

"It's my homework," I said, shocked that she didn't remember that she had given me a special assignment the very first day of school.

Ms. Sugarman unfolded the paper and started to read it. It wasn't very long.

When she finished, she gave me a strange look, and then she smiled. "Do you mind if I share this with the class?" she asked.

I shrugged. I've never liked the word "share." In kindergarten we got in trouble if we didn't share our toys.

Ms. Sugarman frowned.

"Now what's wrong?" I asked.

"Nothing, Jackie. I just wish you didn't shrug so much. This is a very good piece of work."

I walked to my desk as if I were floating. Ms. Sugarman's words rang in my ears: "A very good piece of work."

"You're grinning," said Shannon as I sat down. I started to shrug. Then I stopped myself.

"Girls and boys," said Ms. Sugarman, "before we begin work, I'd like to read something that Jackie Milanzo wrote."

"How can you read it?" asked Seth. "Last year Jackie had the worst cursive writing in all of the third grade."

"I can read it fine," said Ms. Sugarman. "Jackie has a real flair for poetry."

Ms. Sugarman started to read. I could feel my face get hot. My ears felt like they were burning, and my hands felt clammy.

"The title of the poem is 'Naaa,'"said Ms. Sugarman.

The class started to snicker. I was worried

that I was going to throw up.

Naaa

"Naaa," said the goat to the sheep.
"Baa," said the sheep.
"You're going to get in trouble
Saying 'no' all the time."
"You think 'baa' is better?" asked the goat.
"You think everything's funny," said the sheep.
Sheeps have no sense of humor.
"Animals who go around always
Making jokes get in trouble," warned the sheep.
"NAAA," said the goat,
But the sheep was right.
The goat got in trouble.
In the Bible when they seperated the sheep
from the goats,
The goats got sent to the devil.
I guess for saying "Naaa."

My dad warned me about fourth grade.
"They seperate the sheep from the goats."
"Naaa," I said. "It won't be so bad."
The goat and I could be wrong.
I hope fourth grade isn't the Last Judgment.

by Jackie Milanzo

16

It was hard to hear my words spoken out loud by Ms. Sugarman. But as she read, the class quieted down. They stopped giggling. I liked listening to the quiet as they heard my words.

Ms. Sugarman went to the bulletin board and put up my poem. "Jackie's poem will be the first piece of work in our Poets' Corner. Jackie, I found that poem touching and funny. You're a wonderful writer."

"I didn't get it," said Seth. "It didn't rhyme."

"Poems don't have to rhyme," said Ms. Sugarman.

"But it was funny," said Willie.

"Poems can be funny," said Ms. Sugarman. "Look at Jack Prelutsky and Shel Silverstein. They're poets and they're funny."

"Jackie's no poet," muttered Seth.

"Yes, I am," I said.

Ms. Sugarman grinned at me. "See, Jackie? Already you've stopped saying 'naaa.'"

5

She's Not Perfect—She Likes Me!

"I had a poem put up in the Poets' Corner," I told Mom and Dad over the weekend.

"Honey, that's wonderful," said Mom. She glanced at Dad. Dad looked up from his newspaper and smiled at me.

"My daughter, the poet," he said, just a little sarcastically, but I think he sounded a tiny bit proud too.

"You never know," I said.

"What was the poem about?" Mom asked.

"Sheeps and goats," I said. I looked at Dad, challenging him to see if he remembered.

"Sheep and goats," Dad corrected me.

"Did I inspire you?"

He remembered. Somehow I thought he would have forgotten. "Did you know that came from the Bible?" I asked him. "Mom did."

"Of course I did," said Dad quickly. I wasn't sure he was telling the truth.

"Are you liking your new teacher more?" Mom asked me.

"She's okay," I said. I started to shrug and then I didn't.

"She said that my poem was creative and touching. In fact, she said that I have a flair for poetry."

"Has she been teaching long?" Dad asked.

"She's the oldest teacher in the school," I said to him. "She's absolutely wonderful. She's the best teacher I've ever had."

"Sounds like Jackie's got her first crush," teased Dad. I could feel myself blush. Sometimes my dad makes me so mad.

"Ms. Sugarman wants to meet us," said Mom. "She phoned to make an appointment for next week."

I felt my stomach do a double flip. Why did Ms. Sugarman want to see my parents? I wouldn't have minded her meeting Mom, but I just wished Dad wouldn't have to go.

"She said that she likes to meet the parents of all the children in her class as soon as possible," said Mom.

"So we'll get to see your poem," said Dad, "and meet this perfect teacher."

"I didn't say she was perfect," I said. "I told you I liked her and she likes me."

"I think it's nice that Jackie finally likes a teacher," said Mom.

"I just wish you didn't have to meet her," I blurted out.

"Jackie," said my mom, "what do you mean by that?"

"Nothing," I said quickly.

6

Made in the Shade

"Ms. Sugarman?" I asked. "Why are you seeing my parents?" Ordinarily I wouldn't have the nerve to ask a teacher a question like that, but Ms. Sugarman seemed different. First of all, she thought I was a poet. Poets' parents shouldn't have to come to school. Poets should be left alone.

"I like to meet all the parents in the first month of the school year," said Ms. Sugarman. "Your parents and I are both part of a team. We want what's best for you."

The idea of my dad and Ms. Sugarman being on the same team gave me the willies. I didn't want to share Ms. Sugarman with

Dad. It was enough to share with Shannon and Seth and the rest of the class.

"Well, my parents are pretty busy," I said. "They both work. I know they agreed to see you, but its gonna be awfully hard on them." I still held out hope that somehow I could cut this meeting off at the pass.

Ms. Sugarman adjusted her glasses. "Your mom was very nice on the phone," she said. "She made an appointment right away."

"Yeah, but you'll meet my dad," I mumbled.

Ms. Sugarman smiled at me. "You wrote about him in your poem," she said. "I'm anxious to meet him."

"Maybe we should take down the poem," I said. "Dad might not like it. He might think that I was making fun of him in my poem."

"I don't think he will," said Ms. Sugarman. "I want both your parents to see what good work you're capable of."

Her words made me feel good, but I was still worried.

I had a stomachache the whole day that Mom and Dad were coming to school.

"Do you want me to stay this afternoon

too?" I asked Ms. Sugarman.

Ms. Sugarman shook her head. "No, this time I'd like to see your parents alone."

I wanted to stay. "I could hang around," I said. "Just in case you need me.

Ms. Sugarman looked down at me. "What do you normally do after school?" she asked.

"I used to go to an after-school program," I said, "but this year I'm old enough to go home by myself."

"Jackie, don't fret," said Ms. Sugarman. "I have only good things to say to your parents. I'll tell you what we talk about."

I bit my lip. The bell rang for the end of school.

Shannon raced me to the bus line. She won. "You're usually faster," she said. "What's wrong with you today? You seem kind of goofy."

"My parents are coming in to see Ms. Sugarman this afternoon," I said.

"My mom saw her last week," said Shannon. "Ms. Sugarman asked her to make sure I read every night. I think that was it."

"What are you worried about?" asked Emily Chang, who is one of Shannon's good friends. "You're the teacher's pet."

"Jackie? A teacher's pet?" said Adam. "Give me a break."

"Yeah," said Seth. "She's more like every teacher's nightmare."

"Ms. Sugarman likes Jackie," said Emily. "I can tell." I suppose Emily would know. She is usually every teacher's favorite. She's pretty, she's smart, and she's talented. She plays the piano better than most eighth graders, and on top of all that, she's actually nice.

"Do you really think she likes me?" I whispered to Emily. "I know she put my poem up, but . . ."

"Relax," said Emily. "You've got it made in the shade this year."

I sank back in my bus seat. I didn't think it was quite as simple as Emily thought, but "made in the shade" sure sounded great.

7

A Poet—Not a Ball Player

I couldn't wait for Mom and Dad to come back from their meeting. I took my basketball outside and tried shooting some hoops. I missed every time.

I dribbled the ball in the driveway, looking down the street every few seconds to see if their car was coming. It was taking them a very long time. It shouldn't have taken Ms. Sugarman more than five minutes to tell them that I was doing great and that they shouldn't worry about me. Maybe they were having trouble believing her.

I saw the car rounding the corner. Quickly I turned my back and dribbled up the driveway. I didn't want them to know I had been waiting for them. I squinted at the hoop, pretending to concentrate. I stood right in the middle of the driveway.

Dad honked the horn. I ignored him for a minute and concentrated. I pushed the basketball up into the air. It hit the backboard, and for a split second it seemed to balance on the rim. Then it went in.

I grinned at Mom and Dad, grabbed the ball under the hoop and got out of the way. Dad parked the car and held his hands out for the ball. "Lucky shot," he said.

I didn't care if it was luck or skill— I was just so glad that it had gone in and he had seen it. Dad took a jump shot from two feet farther than where I had been standing. I just watched the ball go over the rim cleanly.

"Come on," he said. "Try to guard me."

I waved my hands in the air. Dad feinted to the left and then went around my right and shot another basket.

"Joe," said my mom, "give her a break."

Dad grinned at me. "Okay, I'll shoot left-handed," he said.

"So what did Ms. Sugarman say?" I asked,

trying to sound casual and trying not to huff.

"She said to work on your hook shot," teased Dad. He pushed me out of the way with his right hand and made the shot left-handed.

He handed me the ball. "Your turn," he said.

"Ms. Sugarman *did not* talk about basketball," I said. "Come on, tell me what she said."

"She was very nice," said Mom, who was watching us from the grass by the driveway.

I made a face. "Nice" sounded so bland. I wanted Mom and Dad to be knocked out by all the great things Ms. Sugarman said about me.

I tried faking Dad out by going to his right. I knew he thought I would then dribble to the left, so when he went left, I continued right. I got around him, but I was so excited that I missed the basket completely. I grabbed the ball again and I made the shot. Whoosh! It went through the basket without even touching the rim.

"I quit," I said. "I want to quit while I'm ahead." I tossed the ball to Dad.

Dad frowned at me. "I don't like quitters," he said, dribbling the ball slowly.

Mom put her arm around me. "Ms. Sugarman showed us your poem," she said. "I thought it was cute."

"You spelled 'separate' wrong twice," said Dad.

I ignored Dad's crack. "It wasn't supposed to be cute," I shouted at Mom. "It was supposed to be touching and funny, the way Ms. Sugarman said."

"Don't shout at your mother," said Dad.

"And I'm not a ball player. I'm a poet," I shouted at Dad.

"You're going to be a young lady in trouble, if you don't lower your voice," said Dad.

I sighed. "I'm sorry," I said.

Dad smiled at me. He tossed the ball to me. "Come on," he said. "I'll not only shoot left-handed, I'll spot you five points."

I didn't want to play basketball, but I didn't want Dad to be mad at me. So I played.

8

Wacko Tacos

"I met your mom and dad," said Ms. Sugarman at the beginning of the next week. "They seem very concerned about your schoolwork."

"I know," I said.

Ms. Sugarman smiled. "I told them that I thought you were going to do fine in fourth grade. In fact, I bet you're going to have an excellent year, and that's what I told them."

"I think Dad wishes you had said that I have a terrific hook shot," I told her.

"I don't care about your hook shot," said Ms. Sugarman. "I care about you."

"Yeah," I said, "I know. You and Mom

and Dad are a team. You want what's best for me."

"I don't like it when you're sarcastic," said Ms. Sugarman.

"Sorry," I said. I wondered if I sounded just like my dad.

Ms. Sugarman played with her pencil between her thumb and forefinger, the way my dad did. "Jackie, stay a few minutes after the recess bell. I want to talk with you some more."

I considered those very scary words.

"What did Ms. Sugarman want?" Shannon asked me a little later.

"I think I'm in trouble," I said. "She doesn't like my attitude."

"Teacher's nightmare," whispered Seth, who was eavesdropping.

I glared at him. I took my seat. Ms. Sugarman wrote "Whom did Columbus discover?" on the board.

Seth raised his hand. "Indians!" he said.

Ms. Sugarman wrote down the word Indians, underlining India.

"Is Seth accurate?" she asked the class. "Were the people who were here from India?"

Emily raised her hand. "Columbus thought he was going to India, but he was wrong," she said.

"Right, Emily. We are going to study what the Americans were like before Columbus."

Ms. Sugarman reached into a shopping bag by her desk and brought out a dozen red-hot chili peppers.

"Today we're going to make tacos," she said. "Before Columbus discovered the Americas, one of the largest cities in the world was called Tenochtitlán, a beautiful city where Mexico City now stands. It was built on a series of lakes, with temples and marketplaces bigger and grander than anything then in Europe." Ms. Sugarman never stood still when she taught. She was pacing back and forth with a knife in her hand waving it over the chili peppers.

"Jackie, why don't you come up here and help me sort the chilies," she said. "You can pretend that you're a Mexican girl selling chilies in the marketplace before Columbus's time."

"Get your red-hot wacko tacos!" I yelled.

"No Mexican girl would sound like that," said Seth. "She'd be speaking Spanish."

"No, she wouldn't," I retorted. "Columbus hadn't landed yet. Nobody here spoke Spanish."

"Very good, Jackie," said Ms. Sugarman. "That's absolutely true. You would have spoken Nahuatl."

"See?" I said to Seth.

"Still, try to say it in Spanish, Jackie, because after 1500, you would have spoken a little Spanish."

We had been studying Spanish ever since kindergarten. I struggled to find the words. I got as far as *chiles caliente*, when I was saved by the bell for recess. I started to go back to my desk. Ms. Sugarman stopped me.

"Remember," she said, "I want to talk with you during recess."

I had been having such a good time pretending I was selling tacos that I had almost forgotten. "Yes, Ms. Sugarman," I said, suddenly feeling like a lukewarm, soggy chili pepper.

Ms. Sugarman smiled at me. "Jackie," she said, "did it ever occur to you that I might have something good to say to you?"

I shook my head. It hadn't.

9

You Can Be Much More

I waited while the class filed out into the playground.

"Don't worry," said Shannon.

"Taco wackos," muttered Seth as he went out. "No wonder you're in trouble."

"She's not in trouble," said Shannon loyally.

Ms. Sugarman was sorting the chili peppers on her desk. "Come on up here, Jackie," she said.

Ms. Sugarman moved her chair away from her desk and sat down next to me.

"Sorry about the wacko joke," I said quickly.

"It was clever," said Ms. Sugarman. "I

asked you to pretend you were selling, and
ately came up with a great line.
didn't start in the twentieth cen-
w."
," I said.
aid Ms. Sugarman. "I want
be fun."
d that fourth grade shouldn't
nes," I blurted out. "He never
eacher. You make everything

an put her hands on her lap.
That's what I wanted to talk to you about,"
she said.

"Fun and games?" I asked. "I've been
clowning around too much."

"No," said Ms. Sugarman. "I want to talk
about the difference between home and
school."

"I know the difference," I said. "School is
for work. I'm trying this year."

Ms. Sugarman shook her head. "You're
doing fine in school. Fourth grade can be a
great year for you. I love teaching fourth
grade because that's when a lot of kids
become quite independent from what goes

on at home. You can be your own person here. You're not just the person your parents think you are."

I didn't say anything. I didn't quite understand what Ms. Sugarman was saying.

"On the very first day of class, I asked you to find out something, and you went way beyond the assignment. You came back on your own with a joyful, interesting poem. I respect the work that you've done. And this is just the beginning. You can do much more. And if you get stuck, you can come to me. That's what I'm here for."

I could hardly breathe. Nobody had ever talked to me like that, certainly no adult. Adults had always talked about my "problems."

Ms. Sugarman seemed to be saying that I wasn't a problem. I wasn't her nightmare at all—just the opposite.

"You have talent," said Ms. Sugarman. "I believe in it. Now I want *you* to believe in it."

"I don't have a hook shot," I said.

"I told you I'm not interested in your hook shot," said Ms. Sugarman. "I'm interested in your poetry, your writing. You don't have to please your father in my class. He's not here. You don't even have to please me. You have to please *yourself*. That's what I want you to do."

"You mean separate the sheep from the goats?" I asked.

"It's time to move beyond the sheep and goats," said Ms. Sugarman. "You can be much more."

I swallowed hard.

"Ms. Sugarman," I warned her, "have you looked at my spelling lately?"

"Let me worry about your spelling," said Ms. Sugarman. "You worry about being the best Jackie Milanzo that you can be. That's what we're here for this year."

10

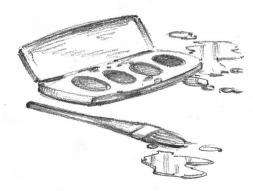

Football Players in the Water

Suddenly I could understand why some kids like school. If a teacher liked you, school was a whole different ball game. I started running from the bus into the classroom, instead of hanging around out in the hallway. I couldn't wait to see if Ms. Sugarman needed my help for anything, like taking back library books or feeding the class gerbil.

One morning, however, Ms. Sugarman wasn't there. The room was empty. Ms. Sugarman almost always came to school early. She told me that she loved the feel of the school when it was just waking up, getting ready for the children.

I hung around the hallway looking for her. Seth was the first one besides me in the classroom. "Where's Ms. Sugarman?" he asked.

"She isn't here," I said, starting to get a little worried.

"Well, don't worry," said Seth. "I'm class president. If she's late, I'll be in charge."

Seth had been elected class president, mostly, I thought, because he wanted it more than anybody else.

"I just hope she isn't sick," I said. "I wouldn't want a substitute." Ms. Sugarman hadn't been sick once all year.

"Yeah, you might not be teacher's pet with a sub," said Seth.

"Shut up, Seth," I said. I knew Seth had been shocked to discover that I was real competition for him this year. Seth was used to thinking of me as a dumbbell.

I heard Ms. Sugarman's voice before I saw her. She was talking quietly to one of the other teachers.

Then Ms. Sugarman turned and came into the room. She smiled at me, but she didn't really look at me the way she usually did. "Is something wrong?" I asked her.

Ms. Sugarman seemed a little surprised by my question. "Take your seat, Jackie," she said gently. "I'll talk to the whole class."

I bit my lip as I took my seat, a little scared that something might really be wrong with Ms. Sugarman.

Ms. Sugarman didn't wait until the morning announcements over the loudspeaker to begin class. "Girls and boys," she said, "I have a sad announcement."

I held my breath.

"Our principal, Dr. Vargas, had a heart attack last night. He's in the hospital. They've told us that he was lucky that he got to the hospital in time, and he should be all right."

I let out my breath. I mean, I was sorry about Dr. Vargas, but I was glad that the announcement had nothing to do with Ms. Sugarman or our class.

"I think it would be nice if the fourth grade made him get-well cards," said Ms.

Sugarman. She handed out paper and water-colors.

"What are we supposed to say?" asked Emily. "I didn't know Dr. Vargas very well."

"That's because you never got in trouble," I said.

The whole class laughed, including Ms. Sugarman.

I hate watercolors. Mine always run together. When I try to draw a sunset, it looks like the sun is falling into a mud puddle. I couldn't think of what to draw. Then I remembered that Dr. Vargas loved football, and the Buffalo Bills were his favorite team. Their colors were blue and white.

I wrote "Hope You'll Soon Be Back on the Ball." I decided to draw a football player carrying the ball through the goalposts.

I outlined the player in pencil. Then I dipped my brush in the water and tried to draw the uniforms, but the blue that I was using for the legs dripped all down the side of the paper. I took my brush and smushed it out.

"What happened to the player's feet?" asked Adam.

"He's running through a stream of water," I said. "I can't draw feet."

Adam giggled. Ms. Sugarman looked at my card and smiled.

"I'm sure Dr. Vargas will like yours," she said. I smiled back at her. I loved Ms. Sugarman's smile.

11

Jackie Goat

Months went by, and I still liked school and I was doing well. This by itself was a minor miracle. It was February, the dead of winter, the time of year when usually I can't wait for vacation—any vacation. But this year was different.

It was snowing out. We made a snow-woman during recess. Ms. Sugarman gave us one of her old woolen hats and a broken pair of her old glasses. Some teachers wouldn't like it if you made a snowperson to look like them, but not Ms. Sugarman.

In the middle of recess, the school secretary trudged out into the snow and waved to

Ms. Sugarman. She handed Ms. Sugarman a note.

Ms. Sugarman walked over to the other teacher on recess duty and said something to her. Then she walked back into the school, even though recess was only half over.

"I wonder what that was about," I said to Emily.

"What what was about?" asked Emily.

"Ms. Sugarman just went inside," I said.

"Her toes were probably cold," said Emily.

"Jackie just has Ms. Sugarman on the brain," teased Adam.

"Ms. Sugarman had a little lamb . . . little lamb," he started to sing, "and everywhere that Ms. Sugarman went . . . the Jackie lamb was sure to go."

"Jackie goat," corrected Seth, grinning at me. "Jackie is Ms. Sugarman's goat."

"I am not," I said.

"Jackie goat, Jackie goat . . ." taunted Seth. "Ms. Sugarman's gonna wake up any day now and realize she's been having a nightmare—making you a teacher's pet."

"I'll get *your* goat," I said. I took a big pile of snow and smashed it in Seth's face. I didn't hurt him, but Seth pretended that I had done him mortal injury. He screamed. Then he tried to tackle me.

The teacher came running. She separated us. "Jackie! Seth!" she said. "I'm ashamed of you. Stop fighting immediately."

Seth and I stood a few feet away from each other, both of us breathing hard.

Shannon held on to my arm. "Don't get in trouble," she said.

"At least they can't send me to the principal's office," I whispered. "It's been a couple months and Dr. Vargas still hasn't come back to school."

The bell for the end of recess rang. "Now, line up to go back to class," said the teacher. "And behave yourselves."

I brushed the snow off my parka and got in line, being careful not to get near Seth. "You shouldn't let him get your goat," said Emily.

I started to glare at her. "Only joking, only joking," said Emily quickly.

I laughed. It's funny how if you like somebody they could say anything to you, and if you didn't, the slightest little jab could set you off. Emily or Shannon could call me Ms. Sugarman's goat and I didn't mind.

We walked back into class. Ms. Sugarman looked as if she had something on her mind that was bothering her. I wondered if she had already heard about Seth's and my fight.

She stood in front of her desk while we put our jackets in the closet.

She gave me a smile, and I felt relieved. Either she didn't know about the fight or she wasn't going to make a big deal out of it. Still there was something weird about the way she was standing. Ms. Sugarman looked nervous, and Ms. Sugarman is almost never nervous.

"Girls and boys," she said. She coughed. We quieted down right away, which in itself was pretty amazing. It was as if we all knew that something weird was going on.

"You all know that we've been without a principal for several months." Ms. Sugarman paused again. So far she hadn't told us anything new.

"Dr. Vargas's doctors have told him that he has to retire early," continued Ms. Sugarman.

I swear she was looking straight at me. "I've been appointed principal," she said softly.

She looked around the room. "It was made official just this morning. The school board approved my appointment."

"Boy, that's going to be a lot of work, teaching fourth grade *and* being principal," I said.

"You dodo," said Seth. "It means that she isn't going to be our teacher anymore."

"He's kidding, isn't he?" I begged Ms. Sugarman. "You don't mean that."

"I'm afraid Seth's right," said Ms. Sugarman. "The school can't function without a principal. I've been in line for a principal's job for three years. We'll find a good substitute for me. But I'm going to have to give up the fourth grade."

"You can't!" I shouted.

Ms. Sugarman gave me such a sad look.

Seth smirked at me. "Too bad, Jackie goat," he whispered.

I hated Seth.

12

Then Good-Bye

I stood on the steps outside school, leaning against the railing. I could feel the cold metal on my hands. I bit the tip of my tongue hard. I stuck out my tongue and tried to look at it, but my nose kept getting in the way.

Shannon came out and stood beside me. "Jackie, what are doing?" she asked. "You look weird."

"Can you believe that Ms. Sugarman won't be our teacher anymore?" I asked.

Shannon shrugged. "Yeah, it's too bad."

"Too bad?" I yelled. "Is that all you can say?"

"Hey, Jackie," said Shannon, "she's just a teacher."

"You don't understand," I muttered.

"You're getting all wired about Ms. Sugarman," said Shannon. "Race you to the bus."

"I'm not taking the bus," I said. "I'm waiting for Ms. Sugarman."

"Why?" asked Shannon.

"I'm going to make her change her mind about becoming principal," I said.

Shannon looked back at me as if I had gone completely nuts.

The bus monitor came and asked what I was doing. I lied and said that my dad was picking me up.

Then I waited and waited. I had to wait until nearly four o'clock before Ms. Sugarman came down the stairs.

"Jackie," she said, "did you miss the school bus?"

I nodded my head. My heart felt like it was beating somewhere up in my neck.

"Is someone picking you up?" Ms. Sugarman asked.

I didn't answer her. "Ms. Sugarman, you

can't be principal," I blurted out.

"Oh, Jackie," said Ms. Sugarman, as if she understood exactly what I meant.

"Please change your mind," I begged. "Get somebody else to do it."

"Did you stay just to tell me this?" Ms. Sugarman asked.

"I'll quit school if you leave," I threatened.

Ms. Sugarman put her hand on my shoulder. "You can't quit school."

"I don't care if they send the police after me. My dad's a police officer. I won't go back."

"Fourth grade is awfully young to drop out," said Ms. Sugarman. I could feel my lower lip trembling, and my eyes felt weird and scratchy.

"Do you want me to give you a ride home?" Ms. Sugarman asked.

I shrugged.

Ms. Sugarman sighed again. "You haven't shrugged in a long time. Come on."

Ms. Sugarman's car was a mess. The backseat was full of books and papers. I had my arms crossed against my chest. Ms. Sugarman wouldn't start until I put my seat belt on. "I don't care if we have a car accident," I said.

"Jackie, you don't need to talk like that," said Ms. Sugarman. "I know my announcement was a shock to you." She leaned over and buckled my seat belt.

"You said you loved teaching fourth grade," I blurted out. "You're going back on your word."

"I do love fourth grade," said Ms. Sugarman. "But there's so much I can do for the school, and being principal is something I've worked very hard for."

"You lied to me," I said. "You said that you'd be there for me."

"I'll still be there for you," said Ms. Sugarman.

"No, you won't," I said. "You'll be principal. I'll only see you when I'm in trouble. I'll get in so much trouble, you'll never get rid of me. Seth and I had a fight in recess today. That's just the beginning of the kind of trouble I'll get in."

Ms. Sugarman shook her head. "I hope not," she said. "It would be such a waste of your time."

"Talk about waste," I said, "you're the one who's going to waste the fourth grade."

"That's not true," said Ms. Sugarman.

Ms. Sugarman pulled up in front of my house.

"Is somebody home?" she asked me.

I shook my head. "Mom gets home by five. Dad, a little later. I've got my key."

Ms. Sugarman drummed her fingers along the steering wheel. "I wish I could think of something to say that would make it easier for you."

I glared at her. That was the first stupid thing I had ever heard Ms. Sugarman say.

"There's only one thing you could say . . . that you're going to keep on being my teacher."

"I can't say that," said Ms. Sugarman softly.

"Then good-bye," I said. I slammed the car door.

13

Nobody Cares About Me

I went to my room and lay on my bed. I counted the icicles hanging down from the drainpipe outside my window. When I'm alone and upset, I always try to count something to calm me down.

I heard the sound of a car in the driveway and the garage door going up and down. I heard Dad's heavy footfall downstairs in the hallway. He was home before Mom. I hadn't wanted him to be first.

"Jackie," he yelled, "are you home?"

I didn't answer. I closed my eyes tight and pretended to be taking a nap.

Dad yelled again, his voice so loud that

there was no way I could have really slept through it. He burst into my room.

I rubbed my eyes as if I had just woken up. "Huh . . . huh," I mumbled.

"I was worried," said Dad. "I yelled and I thought maybe the school bus had gotten stuck in the snow."

"I was sound asleep. You woke me up," I said grumpily.

"Well, don't get up on the wrong side of the bed," teased Dad. He mussed my hair.

"Don't mess with me," I warned him. "This has been the worst day of my entire life."

Dad gave a little half laugh. "Your entire life, eh?" he said, sitting down on my bed, half squashing one of my stuffed animals, a bunny that I'd had since I was a baby.

I pushed him away and grabbed my bunny. "You never look where you're sitting," I shouted at him.

I waited for him to yell at me for yelling at him.

He surprised me. He didn't.

"So why was this such a bad day?" he asked.

"Where's Mom?" I mumbled.

"She'll be home soon. She went to the market. What happened today?"

"I got into a fight with Seth Matthews," I said.

"Did you win?" asked Dad.

"Not exactly," I said. "It wasn't a winning or losing kind of fight."

"You shouldn't fight boys," said Dad.

"Oh, give me a break," I said. "You're the one who taught me to fight."

Dad shrugged. I wondered if I got my shrug from him.

"Don't shrug at me," I snapped. I knew I was going to get in trouble for sass.

"What *is* wrong with you today?" Dad asked.

"Ms. Sugarman is leaving," I said. I could feel the tears. My tears don't start in my eyes. I feel them first somewhere deep in my throat.

"Leaving?" asked Dad.

"She's going to be principal," I said. I swallowed and rubbed my nose with my sleeve.

"Don't do that," said Dad. "Use a tissue."

"Who cares if I get snot on my sleeve?" I said.

"Your mother," said Dad. He handed me a tissue. "I would think that getting to be principal is kind of an honor."

"It is not!" I screamed at him at the top of my lungs. "You don't know anything!"

Now I knew I had gone too far. "Jackie, lower your voice," Dad warned. "You're getting all upset over nothing."

"It is not nothing!" I yelled.

Dad stood up with his hands on his hips. "Stop screaming," he said in a low voice.

I hugged my bunny to my chest. "I hate you," I mumbled into my bunny's ear.

"What was that?" Dad asked. I knew he had heard me.

"Nothing," I said.

"Well, pull yourself together before your mother gets home," said Dad. "I don't want her to see you so upset."

Dad closed the door to my room. I threw myself down on the bed. I could feel the tears streaming down my face. I was blubbering so hard I couldn't see. I hated them all. All Dad cared about was not upsetting my mom. All Ms. Sugarman cared about was her stupid promotion. Nobody cared about me!

14

You're All Sheep

I made a vow to myself not to talk about Ms. Sugarman to *anyone*. In fact, I wasn't even going to talk *to* Ms. Sugarman—only if she called on me.

She told us that she would be leaving in two weeks.

"I just don't see how you can do this to us," I burst out, without thinking. I broke my vow in two seconds flat—so much for my power to do *anything* right.

"I wish I could have given the class more notice," said Ms. Sugarman, "but there wasn't time. I love teaching fourth grade, but I needed a new challenge. And they wouldn't let me wait until the end of the year. I tried to postpone my promotion. We have a very good substitute lined up. I know this class is going to be fine."

"The school was doing fine without a principal while Dr. Vargas was sick," I argued.

Ms. Sugarman shook her head. "That's just not true," she said. "I'm sure you'll like the new teacher."

I snorted.

Later, Seth came up behind me. "I've called a class meeting for recess," he said. "I told Ms. Sugarman that we had to meet in the classroom without her. We've got to do something about Ms. Sugarman's leaving."

"I'm behind you," I said. For the first time, Seth might have a good idea.

Seth smiled. I wish I could say it was a nice smile, but Seth's upper lip never moves when he smiles. It isn't a pretty sight.

It was sleeting during recess. Ms. Sugarman left the room. Seth went to the front and rapped on Ms. Sugarman's desk for attention.

"I've called this meeting because *I* think

we should have a going-away party for Ms. Sugarman. I propose that we have punch and cookies on her last day. We can bake *sugar* cookies."

Seth sounded as if he thought he was being extremely clever.

I raised my hand. Seth ignored me.

"Sugar cookies," he continued, "for Ms. Sugarman. Does everybody get it? We can invite our parents."

I glanced around the class. Everybody looked as glum as I felt. I couldn't believe that Seth was suggesting that we just have a party, as if there was something to celebrate.

"Seth! Seth!" I shouted.

"I haven't called on you yet," said Seth. "We have to go by the rules."

I looked around the room again. Nobody else had a hand up. "Seth, listen to me," I blurted out. "There's nothing to celebrate. Ms. Sugarman shouldn't be principal. She belongs in the fourth grade."

Seth rolled his eyes to the ceiling. "Jackie, grow up, will you? Ms. Sugarman's going to be principal and there's nothing we can do about it. It's a done deal. Don't be stupid."

"Baa," I said.

"What does that mean?" Seth asked.

"Sheep never fight back. I think we should do something to try to keep Ms. Sugarman in the fourth grade."

"Like what?" said Adam sarcastically.

"I don't know," I said, sitting down. "Can't anybody else think of something?"

Emily raised her hand. "Jackie, we're just the kids here. We don't get to vote on who should be principal. At least with Seth's way, we'll get to have a party."

"Emily's got a point," Shannon said.

I wanted to burst into tears. Even Emily and Shannon were ready to give up. I had promised myself that I wouldn't cry again.

I rubbed my eyes. Shannon saw me and looked shocked that I might cry. I almost never cry when anybody can see me. "Jackie, are you okay?" she whispered.

I shook my head. "I am *not* going to let Ms. Sugarman leave," I said.

"What are you going to do?" Seth asked sarcastically. "Chain her to her desk?"

I rubbed my eyes again. Now there was an idea.

15

"Should" Isn't My Word

I rummaged around in my bottom drawer. I was sure that I had what I needed, toy handcuffs that Dad had given me when I told him in first grade that I wanted to be a police officer. Dad had made a crack about police officers being required to know how to tie their shoelaces. Mine were always coming untied. But I think secretly he had been pleased. My grandfather was a police officer, and I would be carrying on the family tradition. But if I went through with my plan to stop Ms. Sugarman, it might mean that I'd never get in the force. Maybe it would go on my permanent record.

I didn't care. But first I had to find my handcuffs. I hadn't played with them in a long time.

Dad knocked on my door. "Jackie, you're going to be late for the bus," he said. "Come on down and have breakfast."

"In a minute," I said. Dad opened the door.

"Your room is a mess," he said.

"I'll clean it up after school," I said. I went to my closet and began throwing things that had fallen on the floor out into the middle of the room. My hands touched something cool and metal.

"You won't be coming right home from school today," said Dad.

I looked at him guiltily. Could Dad read my mind? I grabbed the handcuffs, but I didn't pull them out of the closet. I covered them with a sweater and quickly shoved them both into my knapsack.

"What do you mean I won't be coming right home?" I asked. "I'll be home on the bus."

Dad chuckled.

I grabbed my knapsack. Dad followed me

downstairs. I sat down and slurped my orange juice. I couldn't wait to get to school.

"And to think, two weeks ago you were a basket case about this," said Dad.

"What are you talking about?" I asked him.

"Ms. Sugarman's leaving," said Dad. "Have you forgotten that your class is having a party for her? Mom doesn't think she can get away from work, but I've got night duty tonight. I'll come."

"Oh, that," I said, trying to make my voice sound normal. Dad gave me a funny look. Mom had made pancakes. Her pancakes are a lot better than her granola.

"You don't really have to come to the party," I said to Dad. He was the last person I wanted to be at school today.

"I don't *have* to, I want to," said Dad. "I kind of liked your Ms. Sugarman."

I scowled. She wasn't *my* Ms. Sugarman anymore. Dad ruffled my hair. "Poor Jackie is in a bad mood because her favorite teacher got kicked upstairs."

"Don't tease Jackie," said Mom. "This is a hard day for her."

I looked up at Mom. She rarely tells Dad not to do something.

I finished my breakfast, put on my parka, and took off for school. I knew that Dad's coming *should* make me change my mind about my plans. But "should" was a Seth Matthews kind of word. It wasn't mine.

16

What Are You Going to Do About Jackie?

Ms. Sugarman was dressed in a flower-print dress for her last day in our class.

"Good morning, girls and boys," she said.

"Good morning, Ms. Sugarman," said everybody—except me. I kept my mouth shut.

Ms. Sugarman wrote the words, "I love/I hate" on the board.

"Today, I thought we could all write poems that will tell your new teacher, Mr. Ganey, what you are like. Here's an example that I wrote." Ms. Sugarman cleared her throat. She sounded a little out of breath. Then she read us her poem.

I love the early morning when the classroom is quiet.
I hate the silence of children when they're frightened.
I love my class to laugh at my jokes.
I hate it when they laugh at each other.
I love the chance to run a school for children.
I hate leaving a class I've come to love.

Ms. Sugarman looked around at us when she finished her poem. I felt her eyes on me. I knew she expected me to be moved by it. But I didn't like it. She was a lousy writer. It wasn't funny. It certainly wasn't touching. If she really loved us, she wouldn't leave.

"Now, all of you write something. It can be silly or serious or both," she said.

I took my pencil and started to write. It didn't take me very long. It was as if the whole poem had been waiting inside me. Ms. Sugarman was just asking for it. She wanted me to do something to stop her.

I love the goats—I think their bold
I hate being a sheep and doing what I'm told
I love Ms. Sugarman when she teaches
I hate her when she's principal and preaches
I hate being a sheep
No teacher's ever going to count me in their
sleep
I'm every teacher's nightmare—and I love it.

I took my poem up to Ms. Sugarman's desk, long before anybody else. I carried my knapsack.

I handed my poem to Ms. Sugarman, and while she was reading it, I opened my knapsack.

Ms. Sugarman put on her half glasses to read my poem. "Jackie," she said. She looked upset. She finished my poem. "You're *not* every . . ."

I didn't let her finish her sentence. I whipped out my handcuffs and snapped them on my wrist.

"Jackie, what are you doing!" Ms. Sugarman's voice actually sounded panicky. Good.

The whole class looked up. I sank down onto the floor next to Ms. Sugarman and snapped the other half of the handcuffs around the leg of her desk.

"Jackie!" Ms. Sugarman yelled. Her voice went way up an octave. It was the first time I had ever heard her yell.

"I'm not leaving until you promise to stay in the fourth grade!" I said defiantly. "This isn't a time for poems. It's a time for action."

"I think that's against the law," said Seth. The entire class jumped up and gathered around Ms. Sugarman's desk. They were all staring at me.

Shannon crouched down beside me. "Jackie, what are you doing?" she asked.

"I'm keeping Ms. Sugarman in the fourth grade."

"How are you doing that?" Emily asked.

"I'm not leaving until she changes her mind. Ms. Sugarman won't want to turn her classroom over to a new teacher if I'm still here chained to the desk, will you, Ms. Sugarman?"

Ms. Sugarman bit her lip. I knew I had her.

"You're going to have to call the police," said Seth to Ms. Sugarman. "Jackie's dad is a police officer. He'll know what to do with her."

"Seth," said Ms. Sugarman, "be quiet." She looked down at me. "Are you all right, Jackie?" she asked.

"I'm fine. As soon as you decide to stay and teach us, I'll let go."

"Where's the key?" asked Ms. Sugarman.

I shook my head.

"Search her," said Adam. "I bet she's got it on her."

"Girls and boys, take your seats," said Ms. Sugarman. She had quite a voice of authority herself. I wondered if she was going to call my dad.

Slowly, everybody went back to their seats. I stayed where I was. I wished I had had time to figure out a better way to do this. The leg of Ms. Sugarman's desk was very short, and I couldn't sit very comfortably. I had to half lie and half sit.

"Girls and boys, Jackie is teaching us a very valuable history lesson," said Ms. Sugarman. "In the early part of the twentieth century, before women could vote in this country, some of them chained themselves to the White House gates. During the civil rights movement, many Black Americans chained themselves to the courthouse steps to prove a point."

I raised my hand. Ms. Sugarman looked down at me. She was making me angry. "I'm not trying to prove a point," I said. "I just want to keep you in the fourth grade."

"Nonetheless," said Ms. Sugarman, "you are still in an honorable tradition of protest."

"I thought it was a new idea," I said, a little disappointed that somebody had done this kind of thing before me.

"All right, girls and boys, keep writing your poems."

"What about Jackie?" asked Seth. "Does she get out of work just because she's pulling this stupid stunt?"

"She finished her poem," said Ms. Sugarman. She read it again. She looked down at me. "Do you want to change it?" she asked me.

"Don't be stupid," I muttered.

Ms. Sugarman sighed. She got up and

pinned my poem onto the Poets' Corner. Then she came back to her desk.

"I thought you hated it," I said to her. I was sorry I had called her stupid and wished I could take back the words.

"I do hate it," she said, "but it's still a very good poem."

"Aren't you going to call the police?" asked Seth.

"Seth, I'm more interested in your poem than in your advice." Ms. Sugarman went back to some papers on her desk. I stayed where I was.

One by one, my classmates handed in their poems. They had to step around me.

"Ms. Sugarman," asked Shannon, "is Jackie going to get in trouble?" She sounded worried.

"I'm not sure," said Ms. Sugarman.

17

Big Trouble

My arms and legs were getting cramped. Ms. Sugarman stepped around me. She handed me my textbook and notebook and told me to do my work as best as I could from the floor. She went on with a history lesson and math. It was very, very weird.

I was sure that at any moment, Ms. Sugarman was going to cave in and admit that I had changed her mind. I could just see her announcement. "Girls and boys, Jackie has convinced me. If a girl like her cares so much that she'd chain herself to my desk, I am going to resign as principal and stay as your teacher."

Only she didn't say those words, and all that was happening was that my hand was falling asleep and tingling, and I had to go to the bathroom.

At lunchtime, Ms. Sugarman let Shannon and Emily bring me my lunch.

"Do you know what you're doing?" Shannon asked.

"Yes," I said.

"I can't believe you're doing this," said Emily. "It's very brave."

"It's weird, that's what it is," said Adam.

"Thanks," I said sarcastically. "Don't you want Ms. Sugarman to stay as our teacher?"

Adam shrugged.

"I wouldn't be able to do what you're doing," said Emily. "I'd be too embarrassed."

Shannon just patted me on the shoulder. "What are you going to do about going to the bathroom?" she whispered to me.

I groaned. "Don't even mention bathroom to me," I said. I knew I wouldn't be able to hold out much longer.

"You're going to ruin our good-bye party," Seth spat at me as he came by.

"It won't be a good-bye party if I win," I

said, but I wasn't feeling as brave as Emily thought.

Ms. Sugarman came back into the room just as Seth finished putting up the "Good-bye Ms. Sugarman" banner right over the desk to which I was chained. Shannon and Emily were whispering together. Then they came over to Ms. Sugarman's desk and plastered a "Keep Ms. Sugarman in the Fourth Grade" sign over Seth's.

Shannon grinned at me.

"Thanks," I said.

"Ms. Sugarman!" said Seth. "Do something!"

"You're right, Seth," said Ms. Sugarman. She knelt beside me. "Jackie," she said, "we have to talk."

"Are you staying?" I asked.

Ms. Sugarman didn't have time to answer. My father's voice boomed through the classroom. "What's going on here?"

I scrunched down, trying to make myself as small as possible.

"I told Ms. Sugarman she'd need the police," said Seth.

Ms. Sugarman stood in front of me.

"Seth," she said in her warning voice. Seth shut his mouth.

My father made his way to the front of the room. "What *is* going on here?" he demanded of Ms. Sugarman.

"Jackie is making a protest," said Ms. Sugarman. "She's chained herself to my desk."

"We're with her," shouted Shannon.

"This is ridiculous," thundered my father. "Why don't you just lift the desk and march her right to the principal's office?"

"Because I didn't want to," said Ms. Sugarman in a quiet voice. "Go read the poem she just wrote."

I felt myself turning a thousand shades of red. It had never occurred to me that Ms. Sugarman could just lift the desk. I felt like an idiot.

Ms. Sugarman turned to me. "Jackie, we really do have to talk, however."

My father came back to Ms. Sugarman's desk. "Well, she got one thing right," he muttered. "She *is* every teacher's nightmare."

"Mr. Milanzo," said Ms. Sugarman, "that was *not* the point of the poem."

76

"Jackie's got sheep and goats on the brain," said Seth.

Ms. Sugarman clapped her hands. "That's quite enough, girls and boys. Be quiet!"

Seth began to snicker as Ms. Sugarman and my dad lifted the desk leg. The handcuffs dangled from my arm. I rubbed it.

"Young lady, you are in big trouble," warned my father.

"They're just a pair of play handcuffs that you gave me a long time ago," I said. "They don't even need a key to open." I could hear myself whining and I hated the sound.

"Mr. Milanzo," said Ms. Sugarman, "I am going to do as you said and march Jackie straight to the principal's office. Perhaps you'll come with us."

"Good," said my father. "I hope the principal will have the backbone to teach my girl a lesson."

"Mr. Milanzo," said Ms. Sugarman, "do you remember who the principal is?"

Dad shook his head.

"Me," said Ms. Sugarman.

18

An Original Spirit

We walked into the principal's office. I had forgotten how big it was. It had two giant arched windows that looked out onto a circular driveway where the buses came in every day. It had room for a desk and a couch and two chairs. It even had its own coffee machine.

Ms. Sugarman motioned us to the couch. "Jackie, I've got to admit you've been one surprise after another this year," she said.

"I'll say that about Jackie," said my father. "She's full of surprises."

I started to shrug and then I stopped myself. Ms. Sugarman stood up. "Mr. Milanzo, would you like to see what I wrote about Jackie for her new teacher?" she asked. "Jackie can read it also."

Ms. Sugarman riffled through a stack of papers on the desk and handed one to my dad. I read it over his shoulder.

"Jackie is creative and full of fun and good spirits. She is beginning to believe in herself. She has a special gift for poetry. She's an original spirit who is a delight for any teacher to teach."

I blinked. "You wrote that before I chained myself to your desk," I said.

"That made me only more proud of you," said Ms. Sugarman.

"Proud of me?" I exclaimed.

"Proud of her?" repeated my father. "It was foolish and disrespectful."

"Mr. Milanzo," said Ms. Sugarman, "if people always did what they were told, it would be a boring and pretty scary world."

"You have some strange ideas for a principal," said my father, but I thought I heard a little respect in my dad's voice.

"Mr. Milanzo," continued Ms. Sugarman, "you have a wonderful little girl. I meant every word that I wrote to her teacher. Perhaps you'll leave Jackie and me alone for a minute. I think she and I have to talk. I'll meet you back at my good-bye party."

Dad rested his hand on my shoulder as he started to leave.

"An original spirit," he repeated to himself as if he couldn't believe it. He shook his head.

Ms. Sugarman closed the door behind him. She sat down at her desk. "It's been an exhausting day, hasn't it?" she said.

"I'm sorry if I made you tired," I said.

Ms. Sugarman shook her head. "Beginnings and endings are always the hardest," said Ms. Sugarman, "whether you're writing a poem or just living your life."

I didn't say anything. All I could think of was that Ms. Sugarman wouldn't be my teacher anymore. I really didn't want any more philosophy.

"I'm *not* leaving school," said Ms. Sugarman. "I'll be a part of your life in fifth grade and in sixth grade.

"I hope you'll come to me when you aren't in trouble," she continued. "I'll be here for you. Maybe I'll even be a part of your life as you go on to junior high, high school, and college. I'd like to be."

I sighed. "Ms. Sugarman, you *know* it won't be the same."

"I know," said Ms. Sugarman. "I think you've learned a lot this year. You know you're not every teacher's nightmare. For me, it's been just the opposite. You're fun to teach, and it's time to give somebody else a chance."

"He'll probably hate me. Some teachers would have called the police if I pulled that handcuff stunt on them."

"They would have to call the principal first, and I'll be the principal." I looked at her. Maybe having Ms. Sugarman as my principal wasn't going to be totally bad. She was right. Nobody stays in the fourth grade forever.

"Weren't you mad at me?" I asked her.

"I knew it wasn't a stunt," said Ms. Sugarman. "There's a difference between smart-alecky and real emotion."

"Like the difference between sheep and goats," I said.

Ms. Sugarman nodded. "Yes," she said. "Although I'd love to see a poem without either sheep or goats from you."

"I'll see what I can do," I said. "No promises. But you won't be my teacher to see my poem."

"You can show them to me anyway," said Ms. Sugarman. "It's your choice. Why don't you go back to the party? I'll be there in just a few minutes."

I walked out the door. Dad was sitting on the bench outside the principal's office. He looked a little bit like a kid. I was surprised that he was still there.

"That's where you have to sit if you're in trouble," I told him.

"I remember," said Dad.

"This school wasn't built when you went to school," I said.

"I know," said Dad, "but the waiting areas of principal's offices all have the same atmosphere. Your Ms. Sugarman is going to be quite an unusual principal."

I thought I heard him being sarcastic again. I couldn't stand it. "Look, you can make fun of anything," I said. "But don't make fun of Ms. Sugarman."

"Who's making fun?" he asked.

"Just don't do it," I warned him.

Dad heard me. I wasn't being smart-alecky. But as we walked back to the classroom together, he kept shaking his head.

"What?" I asked him.

"I just keep seeing you chained to your teacher's desk—that's got to be every teacher's nightmare."

"It wasn't," I told him. "Not for Ms. Sugarman . . . and not for me."

ABOUT THE AUTHOR

Elizabeth Levy has written over fifty children's books, both fiction and nonfiction, including FRANKENSTEIN MOVED IN ON THE FOURTH FLOOR and DRACULA IS A PAIN IN THE NECK published by HarperCollins. Her books have been called "boundary breakers, too much fun to miss,"* and "irresistible."**

"The real Ms. Sugarman in Buffalo, New York, made me feel like a poet," she says, "even though I had the worst handwriting in the class. All my characters have moments when they feel they can't do anything right. This book is for all the teachers who turn things around for those kids."

Ms. Levy made it out of Ms. Sugarman's class, and earned a B.A. from Pembroke College, and a M.A.T. from Columbia University. She now lives in New York City.

*BULLETIN OF THE CENTER FOR CHILDREN'S BOOKS
**SCHOOL LIBRARY JOURNAL